Mrs. There-There's Stories

Written and illustrated by Helena A. Paxton

Contents:

About The Author

Helena Alexandra Paxton was born in Portugal, then raised in Lark Lane, on the edge of Sefton Park, Liverpool - a park that provides an enchanting world for a childhood filled with dreams of magic fancy. The park's shaded brooks, woodland thickets, and the whimsical 'Fairy Glen', became the foundation for the magical wood she would later bring to life through storytelling.

Helena delights in firing children's imagination with her fairy tales. Masterfully weaving the familiar comforts of home with the extraordinary happenings in a wondrous world. Her love for fantasy and natural curiosities has remained a constant thread throughout her life.

Now residing near an ancient woodland in Cheshire, Helena continues to draw inspiration from her surroundings. Her creative and artistic flair has culminated in establishing Mrs. There-There, a charming character born from the same spirit of wonder that shaped Helena's early years.

Introduction

And so, it begins...

Mrs. There-There, as she is known, is a 'storyteller'. She lives in a pretty thatched cottage, surrounded by a beautiful garden in a bluebell dell, on the edge of Hob Hey wood.

There is a cobbled path which leads the way through the garden, edged with colourful, scented flowers. As she brushes the leaves into a pile, Mrs. There-There hums a happy tune to herself, while Marmaduke, her cat, looks on. There will be a saucer of milk for him when she's finished!

If you look carefully around her garden after a rainfall, you may see a few silvery cobwebs, holding droplets of rain which glisten in the sunlight, they sparkle like diamonds. You may also notice fluttery butterflies collecting nectar as they flit from flower to flower. If you're very quiet, you may even spy a little elf or fairy; they are shy by nature and so try to stay out of sight by hiding in such places as tiny mouse holes, or inside large flowers during the day. Oh, and then there are all types of mushrooms, which Mrs. There-There keeps a close eye on because she understands that little fairy folk like to shelter under them when it rains.

There is more than one woodland, and naturally, they are all interconnected by fairy paths, mushroom trails, rabbity runs, and not forgetting those amazing spider web bridges which span the brooks and streams. Of course, they are made extra strong for the purpose of passage by fairy folk, tiny animals, and such like.

Mrs. There-There knows many fairies and woodland creatures; she sees them regularly, especially on a baking day when the irresistible aromas of her perfectly scrummy apple pies, or fresh bread, float out of her kitchen window and waft around her garden.

On such days, Mrs. There-There will bake a little extra, as the evening of a baking day always heralds a new story to tell from the book which rests in the magic trunk, which can be found in her sitting room.

Mrs. There-There is the only person who can open the trunk. The story book within contains blank pages, until such time as Mrs. There-There lifts it out, opens it, then waits for the magic to happen, because she is the official 'storyteller' and was appointed by none other than the Fairy Queen!

Storytellers can make stories come alive, and sometimes pictures will literally jump off pages of a book, right in front of your eyes!

She always makes everyone welcome by serving hot chocolate with warm currant buns baked in her oven, hot buttered toast, and lemonade too. The little fairies and woodland creatures settle down wherever they can find a comfortable place to listen to her soft, velvety voice. They wait in anticipation as Mrs. There-There opens the trunk. The magic dust from within rises up and forms swirls which spin themselves into a glittering globe of sparkles.

Mrs. There-There holds out her hands, palms up, waiting for the sparkles to drift down onto them. She then parts her hands, letting the sparkles fall and settle onto the open book's blank pages, which now rests on her lap.

Letters start to appear upon the page, which then form words, and the words become sentences, until finally, there it is. The story is ready for Mrs. There-There to read to her friends who have been waiting patiently.

Mrs. There-There's story today is about an event that happened in Hob Hey wood. There are many stories; sometimes, when one escapes up the chimney on a cloud of magic dust, it will find its way through a window and into a house, where a curious child, such as you, lives. But it is worth noting, you will only be able to see it if, at some point, you have made a wish for something... and wished really, really hard.

Have you ever done that?

Well, go on, let's do it now...close your eyes, squeeze them tightly shut, and make your wish; let's see if you can see the story...

...Now, if you can
read on, then it's not
invisible to you, so, well
done!

The fairies must have heard you
    and decided to grant your wish.

They don't do that for every child!

Let's take a peek to see which of Mrs. There-There's
    stories are about to be told.

Make yourself comfortable, then we will begin.

Chapter I.
Mr. & Mrs. Trill-de-da and Wow

It was early in the morning - everywhere was still and quiet. A waking blackbird stretched his wings whilst opening one eye to observe the horizon. He saw the sun just rising; it seemed to wink at him with a big smiley face.

It was time.

On a warm night such as this, this blackbird sleeps outside, perched on a branch of a tree called Hollow Oak. This is where he lives very happily with his wife.

After much clearing of his throat, and in a very haughty fashion, the blackbird, now with both eyes wide open, puffed out his chest and placed his finger like wing tips in front of him, dovetailing and flexing each feathery tip. He rose upon his tippy toes, stretching to his full height (which is 7 magic inches, or to you and me, 18cm!).

"That felt good."

He took a long, deep breath and... "Oh, it is good to be alive!" he twittered as he sent forth the most musical, delightful birdsong.

It sounded like the tinkling of trickling raindrops, falling into a fountain of bubbles, whooshing from his bright yellow beak. (He has been known, upon special request, to sing a very good yodel too!)

With a quick preen of his feathers, he stretched out his beautiful wings and flew, swooping upon a passing gust of wind. Once in flight, he glided to his next perch, ready to wake his nearby neighbours, as usual. They depend upon him. After all, he is a very important blackbird... his name is Mr. Trill-de-da.

Mr. Trill-de-da's tree can be found on the edge of a magical fairy wood known as Hob Hey. Many fairies live in this wood, as well as gnomes, pixies, elves, and leprechauns (who can be quite mischievous at times), and not forgetting the little woodland animals. They all speak very well indeed, and they live happily together, minding their own business.

One morning, Mr. and Mrs. Trill-de-da sat eating a breakfast made of toast and jam, with a hot cup of tea, in Oak Hollow.

Oak Hollow is a tall, majestic oak tree, at least 3,000 years old. If you look very carefully, you will see a little arched door and two oval windows. The hollow found in the old tree was just perfect to have been made into creature dwellings.

There are two dwellings altogether. No. 1 is where Mr. and Mrs. Trill-de-da live and can be found at the bottom of the old tree's trunk, and No. 2, where a clever owl lives, can be located further up, but his front door is around the back.

When they had finished breakfast, they decided to fly down to the market in the village, which can be found at the edge of the wood. There were always bargains to be had for the early bird!

The first item on Mrs. Trill-de-da's list is a bag of shortbread biscuits from Mrs. Hedgehog's bakery...mmmmm! As you walk through the shop door, the aroma of newly baked biscuits makes your mouth water.

There is an arch opening in the wall of the shop through which you can peer and watch the biscuits being baked. Mrs. Hedgehog's husband decorates the biscuits by pricking

them with the prickly needles on his back. If you look carefully at the biscuits in your biscuit barrel, you will see the pricked-out holes made by Mr. Hedgehog!

Next stop is the lemonade shop owned by a pixie called Bubbles. It always sounds exciting in his shop because the lemonade is super fizzy and makes the noisiest popping and zinging sounds. As a bubble comes to the surface, it will 'pop' very loudly, exploding out of the glass, and then 'zing' around the room until it magically disappears into thin air!

Outside, there are small mushroom tables, with flowery umbrellas to shade the fairies from the sun and stop their lemonade from becoming too warm!

When they had finished their shopping, Mr. and Mrs. Trill-de-da made their way home through the treetops, stopping now and again to rest on a branch, and chat with other birds, and creatures who were going about their daily chores.

When they arrived home, they found a neatly wrapped parcel on their doorstep.

"Oh!" exclaimed Mrs. Trill-de-da, "How exciting. I wonder what it can be?"

They picked it up and took it inside, then carefully unwrapped it on the kitchen table.

There was a note tucked in one corner which read:

"To whom it may concern,

In this parcel, you will find an egg. In the egg is a surprise. It is an incredibly special surprise because this is a magic egg. It was found in a mossy hollow. Please keep it safe and warm until it hatches. Thank you."

It was not signed by anyone!

"Oh dear!" trilled Mr. Trill-de-da. "Goodness me!" chirped Mrs. Trill-de-da.

They bustled about looking for a warm, safe place for the little egg, which had been placed into their care.

They decided the best place would be a drawer, a nice big bottom drawer, in the large chest in the corner. They lined it with feathers and warm cotton wool, then laid a warm blanket over it all. Oh, how cosy the little egg looked nestled safely in its new bed.

They thought this was all quite intriguing!

After lunch, several fairies from next door visited, as they often do. Mrs. Trill-de-da laid the table with a clean, white linen cloth, ready for a plate of freshly baked biscuits, and a small pot of tea.

There was much chattering, and giggling going on, when their attention was drawn to a faint tapping noise.

Tap...tap...tap. Whinny, the tallest fairy asked, "What is that noise?"

Mrs. Trill-de-da replied "Gosh! How silly of me, I forgot to tell you all about our news!" She proceeded to explain about finding the egg which had been left on their doorstep.

There it was again, but louder this time. **Tap… tap...tap.**

"Oh, we must take a peek in the drawer to see if anything has happened." They all agreed and gathered around the old chest of drawers. Mr. Trill-de-da gently pulled the drawer open; he was very careful as he didn't want to disturb the egg.

To their surprise, the egg had already cracked open and there lay the tiniest baby fairy you ever did see. He was nestled in the middle of the broken eggshell, on a bed of yellow silk.

"My goodness!" they all exclaimed in unison. "We weren't expecting that!"

The tiny fairy looked up at them, blinking in the bright light, and rubbed his eyes with tiny, fisted hands. He gazed at all the happy faces looking down on him, then he smiled the biggest smile. So big was his smile that it stretched from ear to ear. His bright blue eyes darted around the room, taking in his new surroundings.

His first word was… "Wow!"

His next words were… "I'm hungry!"

Everyone laughed and shook each other's hands. "Congratulations Mrs. Trill-de-da, you're the proud Mum of Wow, a new baby fairy."

A cup of warm milk was prepared, and soft bread, spread with a dollop of honey. Wow ate everything up; he really was a hungry fairy.

Mrs. Trill-de-da wrapped him up in a pale blue blanket and placed him back in his drawer, where he fell fast asleep, good as gold.

You see, no one knows quite when, or how, a new baby fairy will arrive. They can appear in all manner of ways because they are magical. Once, a baby fairy was found inside a rose bud. Another time, a fairy was found nestling in an empty acorn shell which was floating down a stream. So, it really was a lovely surprise for them all to find Wow inside an egg!

After the visiting fairies had left, the news of the new baby fairy named Wow quickly spread throughout the wood. It was time for a party!

Magic invitations appeared, flying through letterboxes, and into the hands of all the fairies and little woodland creatures who live in Hob Hey.

Come to the party!

The bunting went up, playfully threaded through the treetops by excited fairies. An extra barrel of fizzy lemonade was ordered, wheelbarrows of chocolate biscuits, and of course, dozens of fairy cakes.

A full moon was organised for extra light, silver-backed moths were invited to shine their silvery wings, and glowworms were asked to glow brightly. Lanterns were polished and lit... and even the Fairy Queen sent her incredibly special magic sparkles to dance around the woodland green where the party was to be held; it would all be very bright.

The party lasted until the first twinkle of a star appeared. As is always the case, this meant it was time for bed. Everyone had enjoyed a wonderful time; it was agreed by all that this had been a very happy, magical party, indeed.

Chapter II.
Paddy, and the lost smile

Mrs. There-There settled into her armchair by the fireside after a pleasant afternoon spent baking; she waited while the usual gathering of fairy folk, and woodland friends, found their comfy place.

As she opened the magic trunk beside her chair, all became still and quiet, the only sound that could be heard was the crackling of the log fire, and the ticking clock on the mantlepiece.

Everyone held their breath in anticipation.

…And then the sparkling, twinkling magic dust began to rise from the trunk. At first, spinning and curling, then gently swishing its way around the cosy room, waiting for Mrs. There-There to open her hands, palms up, ready to receive it.

The dust drifted purposefully onto her palms, settling there and becoming a globe of twinkling lights. Mrs. There-There parted her hands to let the lights fall. As they settled onto the pages of the book which was resting on her knee…the story magically appeared, as it always did.

Mrs. There-There started to speak, in her gentle, soothing tones; all eyes were fixed upon her.

"This evening's story is about Paddy, a little leprechaun. Are you all comfortable? Then I'll begin."

Paddy was taking his usual morning walk from one woodland to another, looking sometimes for mischief, but at other times, to grant a wish he may hear whispered on the wind. That is what leprechauns do!

He decided to visit the local café to enjoy a glass of lemonade, where he met Buck Rabbit. He knew many, many rabbits! Suddenly, out of nowhere, a whispering wish floating on a breeze, swished past his ear, catching his attention.

He heard a little sob coming from within the wish; it was a wish that Paddy couldn't let pass without investigating! So, he followed the whispering wish through the wood, and along a path. The path led to a stream with a little bridge over it.

The wish on the wind had led him to another of his little rabbit friends, named Bushy. He looked very sad indeed.

"Whatever is the matter, Bushy? I heard your wish on the wind and came as fast as I could."

Bushy rabbit looked at him with soulful eyes.

"Oh Paddy," he sobbed, "I have lost my smile. I have no idea where I put it. One minute it was there and the next... it had vanished! Oh dear, oh dear, I wish I could find my smile."

Paddy scratched his head. This was most unusual. He decided to help.

He gave Bushy a warm hug and told him he knew of a wise old owl who might know where to find a new smile to replace the one he had lost.

Off Paddy went. Back over the bridge, towards the distant hills where he thought the wise old owl might live.

When he arrived at the woods, he came to a clearing where he found Bambi playing.

"Hello Bambi, good to see you! I don't suppose you know where I can find the wise old owl, do you?" "Ah, yes, I do," replied Bambi, "but he isn't here. You must go through to the next wood. You will find him outside a large oak tree, where he teaches at the woodland school."

"Oh, that is helpful." replied Paddy. "Thank you." And off he went again in the direction which Bambi had advised.

How many little animals can you see?

After a while, he happened across a large pond where a pixie was fishing; he decided this would be a good place to rest. He sat on an old tree stump and chatted to a few ducks and a squirrel. They talked about Bushy rabbit's wish, and everyone agreed it was indeed a promising idea to ask the wise old owl, as he knew nearly everything there was to know, and if he didn't know it, then it wasn't worth knowing anyway!

After his rest, Paddy continued his journey. He came upon another, smaller pond. He hid behind a tree as he didn't want to disturb the shy frogs who were gratefully offering a lily flower to the cleaning pixie, as a thank you for clearing out their pond.

How many ducks can you see by the pond?

A little further on, he came to the village where his friend lives. He decided to pay him a visit, enjoy another rest, and, if he was lucky, maybe a glass of lemonade too! His friend was delighted to see him. They enjoyed a good chat, a refreshing glass of lemonade, and a fairy cake; Paddy soon felt energised. He bid his friend goodbye, then continued his quest to find the wise old owl. Luckily, his friend had told him about a shortcut which would take him straight to the wise old owl's school.

How many fairies can you see?

When Paddy found him, he explained the whole sorry story. Well, the wise old owl was only too happy to help. He directed Paddy to a little shop in the next woodland that sold smiles of all shapes and sizes.

Paddy set off once again. Finally, he saw the shop in the distance; there was no mistake because the cheery looking shop seemed to be smiling too!

Paddy entered the shop; he studied all the smiles. There were large smiles, small smiles, and grimaces, too. There were bags of chuckles, packets of giggles, boxes of sneers, thimble-sized sniggers, and beaming big smiles in jars. There were guffawing laughs, tinkling titters, exuberant snorts, oh, and not forgetting the half-smirks, which were half price! There was a money-back guarantee for misbehaving smiles, and all smiles were insured for 12 hours. After a good look round, he chose a broad smile from a box of bargain smiles that he'd found on the floor in a corner of the shop.

Paddy explained to the shopkeeper the story about poor Bushy rabbit losing his smile. The shopkeeper felt so sorry for Bushy, that he offered Paddy the broad smile for free because it was for such a worthy cause. Paddy was grateful and told the shopkeeper that this particular smile would suit his friend Bushy, perfectly.

Off he went again, back to his own wood, along the path, and over the bridge, where he found Bushy rabbit, still so glum, waiting patiently for him. When Paddy told him the tale about how he had searched through many woods, and how kind folk had been helping him, and about the generous shopkeeper in the Smile shop…guess what?

*That made Bushy rabbit… **smile**!!!*

"Oh Bushy!" declared Paddy. "You haven't lost your smile after all; you had it all the time! It was hiding in your face! Bushy rabbit was so pleased, his smile became quite broad as he beamed happily back at Paddy.

"Ooooh!" Bushy rabbit exclaimed. "How wonderful, Paddy, I feel so happy now. But whatever shall we do with the broad smile you have in the bag?"

"Well," Paddy said, "let's keep it just in case, as you never know, we may need it in future to cheer up someone else."

And that is what they did! Paddy keeps the broad smile under his hat, so if you know of anyone in need of a smile, who looks a little sad, just whisper your wish on a passing breeze, and let Paddy do the rest!

Chapter III.
Mischievous Elves

It was a bright, autumnal day when Mrs. There-There set off for a few groceries from the village. There were friendly faces to greet, and of course, she enjoyed catching up with any news and gossip they had to share! "Time flies when you're having fun!" commented one of her friends, when they suddenly realised

time was short and scurried off to catch the bakers before all the best cakes were sold.

Mrs. There-There looked at her watch, and then noticed the sky, which was beginning to cloud over. Gone was the sunny morning, so, she decided that she had bought enough necessary groceries to make do till her next shopping day - she would walk home before the rain came. Once home, she unpacked her groceries and donned her pinny, ready to bake a batch of cakes. Baking day always brought fairies and woodland creatures in for story time!

Mrs. There-There washed the mixing bowls whilst her cakes were baking in the oven.

Her little cat, Marmaduke, sat patiently by her feet, purring loudly, hoping for a little leftover buttercream from the cake filling.

The aroma of baking smelt delicious; it wafted out of her open kitchen window and was carried on a passing breeze to float its way around the bluebell dell.

It's story time; everyone is welcome.

This story begins with two rascally elf characters, brothers Ash and Oak (named after the trees they were found under, of course!)

They were always up to some sort of mischief.

One day, on their way to school, they noticed two small bags, which had been hidden behind a tree stump. Ash bent down to investigate one of them. He loosened the string holding it closed, when out puffed a cloud of magic dust!

"Oh!" they both declared, stepping back in surprise. The dust landed on a nearby daisy, making it disappear quite suddenly! They looked at each other with a knowing smile. "We could have lots of fun with this, Oak" said Ash, and they chatted away excitedly; they could be very rascally with such a bag of magic!

Whilst continuing their journey to school they noticed Cyril, the squirrel, burying a few acorns in his autumn larder. They hid behind a tree to wait till he had gone. They whispered to each other, cooking up their naughty trick.

Ash said, "Wouldn't it be fun to sprinkle some of the magic dust on his acorns to make them disappear?!"

Oak replied, "Yes, Cyril would think he had lost them. What a hoot!"

As soon as Cyril had finished, he went on his way. Ash and Oak quickly sprang into action. They tiptoed over to Cyril's buried acorns. Ash uncovered them, then Oak sprinkled a pinch of magic dust from the bag onto them. **'POOF'.** They immediately disappeared, much to Ash and Oak's glee!

They then hid behind a few nearby mushrooms and waited patiently for Cyril to return. He had been searching for more acorns, and when he'd found them, he brought them to add to his secret hoard.

"Ooh!" cried Cyril in dismay as he scrambled around searching for his buried acorns. But there were none to be found.

"I am sure this is the right place." he muttered. He looked very confused as he scratched his head!

Well, Oak and Ash could hardly contain their giggles. They fell about trying to stifle their laughter! But they didn't put Cyril out of his misery, no, they left him searching.

They realised it was time for school, so they snuck away quietly, stuffing their hats in their mouths to muffle their sniggers, leaving a poor, bewildered Cyril.

The headmaster, who is the wise old owl who'd helped Paddy, was at the school door, ringing the school bell, and waiting for latecomers. "You're late!" he scolded. "Go inside and sit down, quietly."

When everyone had settled, the headmaster continued, "Today's lesson is spelling. I want you all to start by copying the alphabet as you see it on the blackboard."

Everyone in class duly picked up their pencils and started to concentrate, except…yes, you've guessed it, Oak and Ash were still too full of merriment to study.

Ash had an idea. "Psst… Oak," he whispered. "shall we play a trick on the headmaster?" "Oh yes," replied Oak. "what do you have in mind?"

"Well," replied Ash, "we could make the blackboard disappear when the headmaster isn't looking."

"What a great idea, brilliant. Let's do it!"

As their lesson progressed, they waited for their chance. It soon came when Oak pretended he needed help to write the alphabet; he asked the headmaster to explain.

While he occupied the headmaster's attention, Ash tiptoed over to the blackboard, then sprinkled a few grains of magic dust over it... **'POOF'** *It disappeared!*

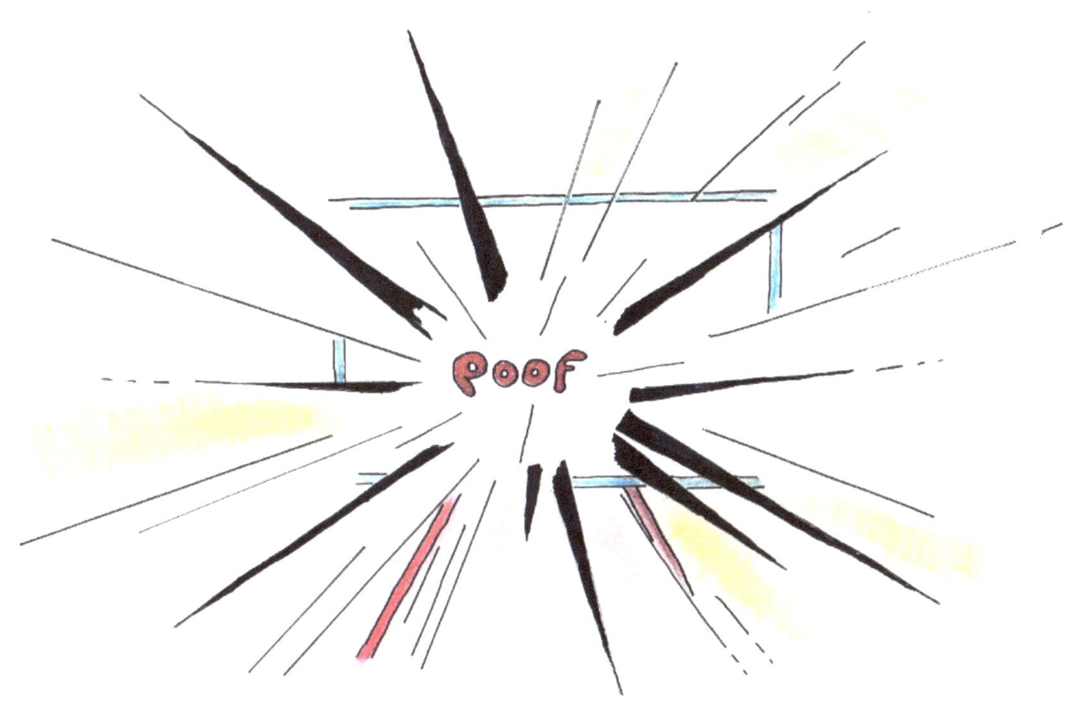

The whole class noticed, and their excited chatter made the headmaster look up... He couldn't believe his eyes.

"Where on earth has the blackboard gone? It was here a moment ago!" he exclaimed.

The headmaster decided to let his pupils leave school early so that he could search for the missing blackboard. Everyone ran out into the sunshine, eager to play, and all agreed that Oak and Ash were the best tricksters in the wood!

It was soon time for dinner; Oak and Ash were quite hungry now as they had missed lunch. Off they trotted home, chatting about their triumphant trickery.

Their mum was waiting for them.

"Wash your hands and sit down, I've made your favourite dinner."

They didn't need telling twice; they raced to the bathroom, each trying to get to the sink first!

When they arrived at the dining table, they looked around for their dinner, but it was nowhere to be seen. Their tummies rumbled with hunger.

"Mum," they said in unison. "where's our dinner?"

Mum came in from the kitchen, hands on hips, with pursed lips. Narrowing her eyes, and giving them her most stern look, she spoke. "Now you two," she scolded, "I have heard a few tales today. I heard Cyril the squirrel was scrambling around searching for his acorns, and then I saw the headmaster searching high and low for his blackboard, and then…I met Sweeney Mugwump, the goblin from the next wood, who had lost one of his bags of magic dust. I guessed you two rascals must have been up to your mischief again when I found a bag of magic dust in your school bag.

Sweeney Mugwump

To teach you both a lesson, I have played your own trick back on you! I used some of the dust to sprinkle on your dinners. They're gone! Now, off to bed, the pair of you."

Oh dear. The two rascals were now feeling very sorry indeed. They went to bed hungry and chatted about ways they could make things right again.

Their Mum, who is always kind, came up to their bedroom later that evening, bringing a plate of supper for each of them. Buttered bread with honey, and hot milk, always goes down well, especially when you're so hungry.

Mum said, "Have you had any thoughts about how you can make amends yet?"

"Yes!" they both said at once. "We will apologise first thing in the morning Mum, but how will we make everything reappear again?"

"Ah," said their Mum, winking at each of them. "I was hoping you would ask me that. Sweeney Mugwump told me there were two bags of magic dust, but you only picked one. The other bag contains the magic dust which makes everything reappear. So, you see, you are not as clever as you thought you were!

Now snuggle down you two, and get some sleep, tomorrow all will be well again, and if you're very good, I will make your dinner reappear tomorrow night."

Ash and Oak slept very well that night, each dreaming of their favourite dinner.

It just goes to show, a clear conscience always makes a good pillow to sleep on!

Chapter IV.
Paddy, and the Whoopee Cushion!

Today's story, as told by Mrs. There-There, is about Paddy when he's naughty, because as you all know, leprechauns can be naughty or nice.

This tale is about one of those days when Paddy was bored, and when he gets bored, he  *can be naughty. That's when all creatures in the wood must watch out!*

Paddy woke up and stretched his short legs. He stuck one foot out from under the warm blankets and wriggled his toes awake. The sun was shining through the round window; he lazily watched specks of dust in the air as they danced on sunbeams. The birds outside were singing cheerfully. They were such happy songs, he decided to shake off his lazy feeling; he would rise and shine just like the sun. This was a brand-new day.

After breakfast, Paddy sat twiddling his thumbs, wondering what he could do. He felt quite bored and thought he may as well go back to bed. Just then, he heard a 'plop' on the doormat. The postman had delivered a parcel.

He remembered he had entered a competition and won a prize from the joke shop, but he had no idea what it could be.

Excitedly, he picked up his parcel and took it to the kitchen table to unwrap. When he opened it, he looked at it in wonderment. The tag inside the parcel read: 'Whoopee cushion'.

"Whatever is a whoopee cushion?" he muttered to himself. He picked it up and gave it a squeeze…

"TRUMPY PUMPY" and again… "ROOOOTY TOOOOOTY" … then "PHBBBTY BRRRRRT" …and a final "POOPY BRRRRPPPTTT"!

Paddy laughed as he realised the whoopee cushion made the best farty sounds!

He started to skip around the kitchen table, making really funny, gassy, fluffer-doodly, poopy-tooty noises. Paddy was no longer bored. "I can have fun with this today!" he exclaimed.

He quickly dressed, picked up his whoopee cushion, and hid it under his hat. Closing the door behind him, he set off for his morning walk through the woods, looking for unsuspecting friends to play a trick on.

After a short while, he arrived at a pond where he saw Freddy, one of the shy frogs.

"Good morning, Freddy. How are you today?" Paddy asked, trying to hide his mischievous smile.

"I am quite well, thank you, Paddy." Freddy replied.

Paddy scratched his head, wondering how he could get his whoopee cushion under Freddy without him noticing.

Then, he had it…

"Freddy, I wonder, would you mind if I sat on a lily pad next to you?"

"Not at all." replied Freddy, trying to hide his shyness and be brave. He pulled up a second lily pad for Paddy. As he did so, quick as a flash, Paddy managed to sneak the whoopee cushion under shy Freddy's bottom.

Well, as unsuspecting Freddy sat down, there was an almighty F A R T Y noise!

Freddy's eyes popped! He shot off the lily pad and landed in the long grass. He peeped out, "Oh goodness me!" he cried, "However did that happen? I do apologise, Paddy, I didn't know that was coming. Oh dear, Oh dear. how embarrassing."

Paddy began laughing so hard, he nearly fell off his lily pad into the pond!

It soon dawned on Freddy that Paddy had played a trick on him, so although he was relieved that he hadn't actually rooty-tooted, he felt quite annoyed with Paddy. He told Paddy so, and in his shy, frog-like way, he muttered, "You are a naughty leprechaun."

But Paddy didn't care, and off he went, still chuckling as he skipped away, leaving a subdued Freddy the frog.

He spied his next victim up a tree. It was Cyril the squirrel!

Paddy thought he would make an ideal target. You see, Cyril is usually quite a serious squirrel, which meant that Paddy thought it would be good fun to play a trick on him.

"Good morning, Cyril. What a beautiful day it is." Paddy shouted. "I wonder, would you mind coming down from your branch to chat with me for a while?"

"Good morning, Paddy. Of course. I always enjoy catching up on news from around the wood."

Down climbed the unsuspecting squirrel, and guess what? Just as Cyril was about to sit down, Paddy swiftly shoved the whoopee cushion under Cyril's bottom.

"WHOOOOOOSH!" the loudest, longest farty noise echoed around their heads!

The whizz of wind made Cyril's tail uncurl like a spring let loose; it thrust out, straight as a poker!

"Oh no!" cried Cyril. "I do apologise, that big trouser cough was a terrible accident!" He quickly stood up to brush the leaves from his tail - that's when he noticed the whoopee cushion.

"Oh Paddy! I do believe you put that there on purpose. I am so relieved it wasn't me making that big toot. You are a naughty and mischievous leprechaun."

But again, Paddy didn't care one bit. He was having so much fun. He danced away, chuckling, and started looking for someone else to play his trick on.

He soon found a new target. None other than Mugwort, the most somber of all gnomes. He is one of the protectors of the wood and all who live within; he is held in high esteem amongst all fairy circles.

"Good morning, Mugwort" Paddy said as he gave a low, respectful bow. "Good morning to you too, Paddy" replied Mugwort, in his usual gruff voice. Paddy continued, "Mugwort, I wonder would you mind sitting with me for a while and explain how you manage to help protect so much woodland all at once?"

"Well, if you really want to know, I suppose I could tell you Paddy, but you must not tell anyone else."

Just as Mugwort rearranged his coat to sit down on a nearby woodland stool, Paddy whipped out the whoopee cushion from under his hat once again, and in the blink of an eye, yes, you've guessed it, the biggest F R A A A A A A A A A T you ever heard came from under Mugwort's coat.

Well, it blew out his coat, making him look like a hovercraft, and what's more, it whooshed up his floppy hat, making it absolutely straight! His face grew rather red, and he coughed loudly, trying to hide the almighty farty noise. "My word!" Mugwort exclaimed. "I am most displeased with my bottom; it had no right to butt trumpet without my permission." His words were drowned out by Paddy's hysterical laughter. Tears of mirth were rolling down his chubby face, and he held his pot belly as he chuckled and spluttered his giggles. Mugwort realised the instant he saw the whoopee cushion that Paddy had played a rotten trick on him - he was rather disgruntled, and quite annoyed.

He turned to Paddy with a look of scorn. He narrowed his eyes as he scolded him.

"Beware Paddy, you will play one trick too many one day, and then the laugh will be on you. You will be sorry!"

Of course, Paddy wasn't listening; he was off before Mugwort could finish his sentence, and he laughed all the way home.

The following day started much like any other, and Paddy decided that he would visit the café for lunch. He whistled happily as he made his way there through the woods. On arrival, he sat down to read the menu. He was surprised to see it had been changed — there was a new pie, and it contained his favourite vegetable, Brussel sprouts; it was being served with delicious baked beans in tomato sauce.

"I have never tasted sprout pie with baked beans before. I really must try that one."

He went to order his meal at the counter.

What he didn't know was that Freddy, Cyril, and Mugwort, were hiding behind the door at the back of the café. They had got together and conspired to teach Paddy a lesson! They knew that he loved sprouts, and baked beans too. They also knew something Paddy didn't, which was that if you eat too many sprouts and baked beans, it creates the most massive rooty-tooty, blow-off noises you ever did hear, only this time, real ones, and if you ate too much of it all, the poopy whizz-bangs could last for days, and days, and days! They had asked the baker to bake such a pie, with plenty of sprouts, served with gallons of baked beans.

Now it was their turn to giggle whilst they watched Paddy tuck into his lunch. He enjoyed it so much, he went back and asked for seconds! He washed it all down with a large glass of fizzy pop – another guaranteed fart maker! All those ingredients mixed together were becoming quite turbulent in Paddy's tummy. He pushed back his hat and rubbed his pot belly, which was now making noises like a grumbling volcano ready to erupt! His face became rather red, and then quite pale!

"Oh Oh, this doesn't feel good." Paddy muttered... "I think I need to make my way home, sharpish!"

But it was too late. As Paddy stood up, he certainly didn't need a whoopee cushion... his trousers exploded with a powerful bottom burb which nearly broke the chair and split his trousers!

"Whoops!" He rushed to the gate. The next bottom explosion blew him up into the air!

His hat was blowing off whilst he hiccupped and burped very loudly. In fact, his sprouty, beany, fizzy wind was propelling him up the hill faster than he could run!

One of the almighty explosions blew a great hole in the back of his trousers, exposing his polka dot underpants!

Paddy was last seen galloping at great speed over the hill toward home.

Freddy, Cyril, and Mugwort, couldn't help laughing as they watched Paddy's hasty retreat. They suspected Paddy wouldn't be playing any tricks like that on anyone, ever again! It served him right, they thought.

When Paddy had recovered, which took quite some time, he realised that his prank hadn't been very nice after all; he pledged to apologise to everyone and burst the whoopee cushion so it could never fart again…

   …But not until after he had squished it one last time!

It let out a final, gigantic WHOOOOOMFFF…and then all became quiet once again in the woodland.

For now, anyway!